R0200371854

07/2019

O9-BRZ-338

Dear Parents:

Congratulations! Your child is taking the first steps on an exciting journey. The destination? Independent reading!

STEP INTO READING® will help your child get there. The program offers five steps to reading success. Each step includes fun stories and colorful art or photographs. In addition to original fiction and books with favorite characters, there are Step into Reading Non-Fiction Readers, Phonics Readers and Boxed Sets, Sticker Readers, and Comic Readers—a complete literacy program with something to interest every child.

Learning to Read, Step by Step!

Ready to Read   Preschool–Kindergarten
• big type and easy words • rhyme and rhythm • picture clues
For children who know the alphabet and are eager to begin reading.

Reading with Help   Preschool–Grade 1
• basic vocabulary • short sentences • simple stories
For children who recognize familiar words and sound out new words with help.

Reading on Your Own   Grades 1–3
• engaging characters • easy-to-follow plots • popular topics
For children who are ready to read on their own.

Reading Paragraphs   Grades 2–3
• challenging vocabulary • short paragraphs • exciting stories
For newly independent readers who read simple sentences with confidence.

Ready for Chapters   Grades 2–4
• chapters • longer paragraphs • full-color art
For children who want to take the plunge into chapter books but still like colorful pictures.

STEP INTO READING® is designed to give every child a successful reading experience. The grade levels are only guides; children will progress through the steps at their own speed, developing confidence in their reading.

Remember, a lifetime love of reading starts with a single step!

Visit us on the Web!
StepIntoReading.com
rhcbooks.com

Educators and librarians, for a variety of teaching tools, visit us at
RHTeachersLibrarians.com

ISBN 978-1-9848-4805-5 (trade) — ISBN 978-1-9848-4806-2 (lib. bdg.)

Printed in the United States of America

10 9 8 7 6 5 4 3 2 1

Random House Children's Books supports the First Amendment and celebrates the right to read.

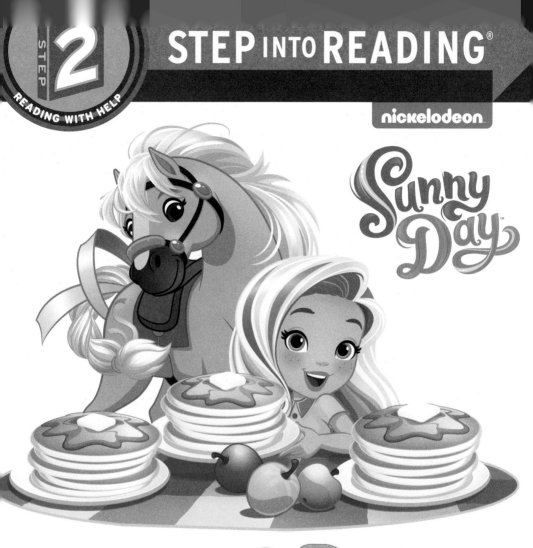

PANCAKE PARTY!

adapted by Celeste Sisler

based on the teleplay by Rachel Vine

illustrated by Susan Hall

Random House 🏠 New York

Johnny-Ray and Suzette
visit Sunny at her salon.

Blair, Rox, Rosie, Doodle, and Violet are there, too.

Johnny-Ray asks the girls
to style Suzette
for her pancake birthday
party!

Rox washes Suzette's tail.

Blair paints her hooves.

Sunny gives Suzette
a ponytail.
She adds a green bow.

Suzette is ready

for her pancake party!

Johnny-Ray needs
to get apples and syrup
for Suzette's pancakes.

He leaves the salon
with Doodle, Violet,
Rosie, and Suzette.

Johnny-Ray and the pets
go into the woods.
They hear a cry for help.

They race over
to a hole in the ground.

They see Timmy
in the hole.

He needs help!

Suzette has rope.
They all try
to pull Timmy out.

Oh, no!

Johnny-Ray and the rope

fall into the hole, too!

The pets look for help.
They find Sunny
and her friends.

Violet tells them
about Johnny-Ray
and Timmy.
Sunny has a plan!

She has extra green ribbon from Suzette's birthday bow in her apron!

Sunny ties one end

of the ribbon to Suzette.

She throws the other end
down the hole.
Johnny-Ray and Timmy
tie the ribbon to the rope.

Suzette pulls hard!

Everyone cheers her on.

Johnny-Ray and Timmy
pop out of the hole.
They are finally safe.

Sunny and Suzette
saved the day!
It's time for the
pancake party!
Happy birthday, Suzette!